Finding My Way

An Autobiography by May McGregor Bourret

Penfield
BOOKS

Dedication

My love to Angela Nejdl (1948–2009) who rescued many fine dogs.

From My Baby Book

Our neighbor Jeanne Olinger took this photograph of me with my new family, Dwayne and Joan. I am three-fourths Labrador and one-fourth French Poodle. Labs came from Newfoundland to England.

Edited by Dwayne M. and Joan Liffring-Zug Bourret, Melinda Bradnan, Alan Brody, Miriam Canter, Dorothy Crum, David Heusinkveld, Julie Jensen McDonald, Rodger Rufer, Kelly Nelson, Deb Schense, Mary Sharp, and Jeanne Wright. Illustrations by Diane Heusinkveld. Photography by Joan Liffring-Zug Bourret unless credited otherwise.

Foreword

We knew in May's puppyhood that she was very special. She was unusually meek, quiet and thoughtful. Now we realize that she has drawn on her talents from a past life, or lives, to create this book. Maybe she was a writer or a poet. Her friend, the Reverend Laura Gentry, a certified laughter yoga teacher, does not believe in reincarnation but suggests that if she did, she would swear May had been a successful comedienne in a previous life.

May reflects on another distinguished dog, Scoshi, who wrote John O'Hurley's book, *Before Your Dog Can Eat Your Homework, First You Have to Do It: Life Lessons from a Wise Old Dog to a Young Boy.*

A live-action NBC television program in 1976 featured *McDuff, The Talking Dog.* McDuff, the ghost of a century-old sheepdog lived in a home owned by veterinarian Dr. Calvin Campbell, the only one who could hear or see McDuff. If you search for talking dogs on the Internet, there is a site featuring different breed speakers.

One famous couple in American literature is Archy and Mehitabel. Archy, the cockroach, was a poet in an earlier life. Mehitabel was a New York alley cat with possible links to Cleopatra. Over a century ago, Archy had access to Don Marquis's typewriter. Archy could reach only the lower case keys to write primarily about Mehitabel. Archy and Mehitabel live on in musicals and in new books. Other talented reincarnated literary creatures also may exist.

While taking a short course for publishers in 1995, I met the late Winafred Blake Lucas, Ph.D. Her book, *Regression Therapy: A Handbook for Professionals* Volume II, features on page 478 a dog, Rama, who, she wrote, would reincarnate in human form. Winafred served on the faculty of Los Angeles State University and later as a core faculty member of the California School of Professional Psychology. She was editor of *The Journal of Regression Therapy* during its formative years. Winafred died at age 95 on Christmas Day 2006. Winafred references reincarnation as a thread in Eastern religious thought and philosophy in her two volumes about Regression Therapy.

As May needed our assistance in creating her autobiography, we were delighted to do so.

—Joan Liffring-Zug Bourret

Preface

I hope this autobiography inspires and helps others, especially dogs who are my friends, dogs I meet in the future, and dogs everywhere as long as they can read and bark.

We should aim high and rise above life's disappointments. I have been helped and inspired on this journey by many souls, particularly by my editors.

This book describes my life during my first year-and-a-half as May McGregor Bourret. Dogs age quicker than humans. One year of human time equals seven years or so for me. As people live longer, maybe I will live longer, extending my service to others.

Most of my growth occurred in my first year. Hopefully, my mission in this life will not be completed for at least another ten years, and I hope my owners live well into their 90s.

Living in Iowa City is inspiring, especially since it was designated a City of Literature* in 2008. Many famous writers have participated in the Iowa Writers' Workshop at the University of Iowa and in the University of Iowa International Writing Program. Both attract writers from all over the world to Iowa City. I feel humble just thinking about them.

—May McGregor Bourret

*Bestowed by the United Nations Educational
Scientific and Cultural Organization
(UNESCO)

Contents

May Day...7

Hairstyles and All About Tails....................9

Life With Sister April...........................12

Jealousy...13

Respect and Submission...........................14

Gypsy: The Newest Dog on the Block...............16

All About Papers.................................19

Manners..20

A Wild Dog.......................................21

Politics in the Dog Park.........................23

A Lover Propositions.............................24

A Whisper from April.............................29

Photographs of People Who Sleep with Their Dogs...30

In Remembrance of April..........................65

Posing for My Modeling Career....................68

Laughter Yoga for Dogs...........................88

My Favorite Recipes: Homemade Treats............106

Epilogue..111

My Favorite Positions
My Favorite Toy: A Squeaker

May Day

My name is May McGregor Bourret. I was born July 1, 2007, along with nine siblings of questionable parentage. In fact, I do not know where to find them. At this point there is nothing to gain by getting a court order to open sealed adoption records.

My dad was a Labradoodle, likely a golden, and my mother was a black Labrador. By design, my mother should have been a Poodle, but maybe most Americans can not trace parentage too far back. The owner of the Labrador looked at us and decided to take us to the pound, another word for orphanage. This was certainly a better fate than that of the kittens who were drowned in a garbage can without any holes in the bottom in New York City, as told by a major American writer about Archy and Mehitabel.

All ten of us, half solid black and half with golden curls, were rescued by a woman near St. Olaf, Iowa. After four or five found homes, my new owners, Dwayne and Joan, found me rolled up with the others on a smelly straw pile in the barn. We first saw the light of day when this dog lover's grandchildren played with us outside. Joan and Dwayne wanted a female, and the woman said "only males are left." They came inside the barn to look anyway and after rejecting a golden curly boy, they picked me up and found I was a girl. This woman teaches high school English. Dwayne said, "It's lucky you are not teaching sex education." Due to my questionable background, I cost a mere $75 instead of $500 for the female designer Labradoodles listed in Sunday advertisements under Pets. Some Labradoodles on the Internet are $1,500. Joan didn't care because she had already adopted a dog, April, whose background was even more disturbing than mine, a dog no one would consider a "designer" dog.

April's mother was a registered golden Lab living in a garage in Methodist Hollow, on a hilly street past a church in McGregor, Iowa. She was wooed at the end of her chain by a passing Border Collie resulting in ten round fuzzy puppies: five boys, five girls. Joan came on her bike to check this litter and found the only pup who would snuggle. This was April, my adopted older sister, now age twelve, who hated me at her first glance of me in the arms of Joan. Now you know my credentials and what little there is to know of my pedigree. Next, all eight pounds of me entered my new home.

Hairstyles and All About Tails

Poodles have tight curly hair. "I just can't do a thing with my hair," is their lament. Labradors have short straight hair. Labs shed; Poodles do not.

I had straight black hair, and I met the women's fashion trends of late summer 2007 with only the hint of curl at the end of my very long tail, which was almost as long as my body.

My friend, Mary Lou, told Joan to have my tail docked. Joan said, "There is enough pain in life without having surgery for a shorter tail, just because Don and Mary Lou's German Shorthair Pointer, Shadow, has one." Shadow having a bobbed tail doesn't mean I have to keep up with the neighbors. This is a waste of time and in some cases gas. So far, I've only knocked over a flower pot on a low stand, and it didn't break. I feel good and want to have all the tail possible.

After three months, I was getting pronounced waves in the hairs on my back and a little fuzz at the edges of my legs. Wait and see what happens next is our family's policy regarding coiffures.

Although Joan gets her hair curled to please Dwayne, I won't change my hairstyle to please a male French Poodle, or male Labrador, or male Labradoodle. Given my French ancestry, I want to be in high fashion. Joan had French-speaking ancestors. She prefers blending with the crowd, with the exception of pleasing Dwayne.

Miriam, a food editor with our family's publishing company, noted that women with naturally curly hair are getting their hair straightened. At four months, the hair on my back is getting longer and longer and is possibly changing from waves to curls. I don't think I should ask for blond highlights. My toenails are trimmed, and I prefer leaving them natural instead of colored. Many of Joan's friends in their late sixties to eighties have painted toenails!

I don't know if the vet will straighten my new Poodle curls or paint my toenails, even if I ask. I'll have to wait for a visit to one of the posh puppy spas.

My Rebellion Begins.
Who is in Charge of Me?

If I Can't See Them, How Can They See Me?

When Dwayne told me to go back to my kennel in the basement, I hid in the corner by the kitchen door.

Life With Sister April

When seventy-five-pound April was introduced to me, she snapped at me, drawing blood. I screamed. Joan and Dwayne ordered me to avoid April. So much for the theory that an old dog can teach a new dog anything. It was three days before April would make eye contact with Joan.

April turned her head and wouldn't look at me. She escaped by going down a circular stairway to a lower level of the house. Even though I weighed sixteen pounds at three months, going down stairs was scary. I am like lightning going up stairs to see if April had left any food in her bowl. What a treat! She liked to eat half immediately, leaving some for later. Save for later? Not if I can help it. My interests are eating, chewing and digging the ferns. Bird bath water beats tap water.

April finally made up with Joan, and I slept in the living room with April by the fireplace. I licked her ear in the kitchen without provoking violence. Joan and Dwayne now wonder if they are too old at seventy-seven and seventy-eight to have a puppy, but it is too late, isn't it?

April, Dwayne, and Joan enjoyed boating at Lake Kabetogama.

Right: Dwayne and April are on our McGregor driveway. April had Labrador Newfoundland ancestors, and her Border Collie ancestors came from Scotland.

Jealousy

We enter this world with wide-eyed faith in our surroundings and love for those dear to us, but the world is not always a huggy place. Being part Poodle, I like giving love, and I expect to receive even more back.

April ignored me. When I had to live for twenty-one days with relatives, Artie and Diane, office staff said April was happy being the ONLY dog in the house. I lived free of fear those weeks. I got to know woods, leaves, twigs and squirrels. When April vacationed there, a squirrel made the fatal mistake of running up a hill instead of a tree. April made her second kill.

Previously she demolished a young raccoon, and she remembers the big raccoon who nearly drowned her in the Mississippi River. Raccoons did-n't have a second chance with April. Dwayne rescued April by using a two-by-four to knock that raccoon off her back. Raccoons drown dogs by holding their heads under water. I do not plan to ever kill another living creature. It is not in my nature from any past life.

When I came home, April was nicer to me. We both rode in the back-seat of the car, without an attack. I am almost half her size. Just wait!

Rebel Heusinkveld

Rebel enjoys her ancestry of Beagle and German Shepherd. Beagles originated in France.

Dwayne and Joan fed April treats first because she's the Alpha dog. I am too filled with love and hope to care. This morning I played with Rebel, a dog belonging to relatives, Carol and David in Amana. When Carol patted me, Rebel growled. Rebel deferred to April, the older Alpha dog. Rebel is half Beagle and half German Shepherd. I spend a lot of time lying upside down in Rebel's company.

In how many homes do younger sisters lie upside down for older sisters or cousins? Joan said that in her mother's family her aunts in their eighties and nineties were still jeal-ously competing for possessions.

Respect and Submission

Once April was used to me, I certainly didn't go upside down for her; but when a dog is bigger, it's safest to immediately go flat on my back! I go belly up for tiny aggressive dogs. They characterize me as "timid," and I hope to outgrow this behavior.

It is safer that way. As far as I know, money determines the status of human systems. I do not know all the ways they show deference to one another, but it is not by going upside-down. Humans also measure status from organizations and their various pedigrees.

According to Internet genealogists, President Barack Obama will always be vertical because he shares seventeenth century ancestors with former President George Bush and Vice President Cheney. As an American pooch, I practice barking as needed; I know my name is May, and the word "come."

In the canine world, size determines who goes horizontal, usually after sniffing. I've been practicing with my squeaky ball. I can flip over quickly, especially when I meet other dogs.

Because I come when called, maybe they won't send me to obedience school. I hate being flat on my back around those bigger dogs. Flattening my body degrades my French ancestry. Joan and Dwayne visited France and report that the French prefer to speak French and have few signs, if any, in English. Because they do not pick up dog poop when they walk their dogs, one must step carefully, particularly in Paris.

Before I was born, a Chinese doctor lived in our house. She taught April commands in Chinese, but April forgot everything she learned as she grew elderly.

I prefer the company of young dogs like McGregor Olinger, also of mixed ancestry. He runs with me, and I can forget upside-down submission. I do not understand the status of so-called purebred dogs. We are all descendants of wolves whether we howl or not.

Editor's note: Shadow's ancestry comes from a mix of a Spanish Pointer with the German Hanover Hound, later mixed with the English Pointer. She is truly European. Like many of the sensitive members of her breed, she insists on living in the house.

Mr. Hattery tenderly protected me while Shadow sniffed.

I turned upside-down for Shadow Hattery, an elderly German Shorthaired Pointer. My heart beat very fast. Shadow is much larger than my half-sister April. Shadow found me very boring.

Gypsy: The Newest Dog on the Block

After putting Shadow down due to infirmities of old age, the Hatterys were lucky to find Gypsy to share their lives. Mr. Hattery wrote the following about her.

Dear May,

Gypsy came to share our home on September 22, 2008. She is a German Shorthaired Pointer and tells us that she will celebrate her fifth birthday on July 4, 2009. Her life to date has been rather nomadic, hence her name. She was born in a suburb of Las Vegas to parents who were part of an act at one of the casinos on the Strip. She ran away from home at an early age to join the Wilder West Circus. There she became a high wire performer of some repute. Tiring of constant travel, she became a fortune teller with a booth in Ghirardelli Square in San Francisco, where her talents were very much in demand.

An itinerant traveler regaled her with tales of the magic of the Mississippi River, and she became captivated. Fortunately for us she answered our ad in the San Francisco Chronicle for an Assistant to the Assistant President of Sny Magill University, and we are delighted that she did. She related to that when she saw that the quote from *Wind in the Willows* where Water Rat says to Mole, "There's nothing half so much worth doing as simply messing around in boats," was an important part of the SNY MAGILL UNIVERSITY* philosophy. She was hooked.

Gypsy took a few weeks off to have a family, and has now joined us. Her duties as Assistant to the Assistant President will be to promote the tenets of our motto "Training Leadership for Yesterday" throughout our influence area.

—Don Hattery, President, Sny Magill University

Sny Magill is a sparkling little trout stream that meanders out of the limestone hills and enters the Mississippi backwaters at the lower end of Johnson Slough in northeast Iowa. Sny is derived from the Scottish name for creek. The Magill family lived along the creek. Where Sny Magill meets Johnson Slough was the hiding place for a band of river pirates.

Sny Magill University President Don Hattery has served as a Commodore of the Upper Mississippi Boat and Yacht Club. He is pictured with his wife, Dr. Mary Lou Hattery, fiber professor, and Gypsy in their river home's great room in south McGregor, Iowa. The river is visible from all their windows. Gypsy is protective of the Hatterys and would not allow me into the house. I will settle this issue with her in our next lives!

Willow Boeder of Marquette and Cedar Rapids, Iowa, is the first dog small enough to play with me without me having to go upside-down in frightened submission. In all my lives, I've been a timid pacifist. Willow is a Wirehaired Terrier, claiming ancestry from England and Scotland.

Handsome McGregor Olinger is a rescued dog with a past. He isn't telling anyone his story. After being rejected from four homes, he is very needy, and he thanks Bill and Jeanne Olinger for his good home. He is game for a run anytime. No one knows his ancestry.

All About Papers

Joan has papers proving a common ancestry with President George H.W. Bush, the elder, and former President George W. Bush, the younger. Joan, the Bushes, and probably thousands of other people in the last 300 years may trace their Penfield lineage to James Upson, a somewhat questionable character who owned the land under Miss Porter's School in Connecticut. He was arrested for drunkenness, a common affliction in that day and ever since. Being part Labrador, I would rather play in liquid than drink it.

Dwayne has papers showing French-Canadian ancestry and possibly an ancestral Catholic priest who crossed the border. Actually Joan also has an ancestor of the cloth, a Catholic priest in Belfast, who fled to Scotland in pursuit of a Scottish lassie just before the American Revolution. A couple of days ago, the Bourret landscaper, Paul, came with Pup, now that Bear has died. Bear had a real life obituary in the *Iowa City Press-Citizen*. Bear knew more than 200 people who provided treats. Bear was mostly Labrador, but who knows what it took to look like Pup. Born in Fairfield, Iowa, site of a college of Transcendental Meditation, Pup's owner Paul said, "Pup learned to meditate but not levitate." Neither dog had papers.

I was so busy annoying Pup that I forgot why they had taken me outside to the new gravel parking. Once back inside, I darted for my favorite paper, *The New York Times*. It was almost a near miss, but I managed to score on top of the photo of a president of an enemy country. Dwayne was pleased because he needed a really good sample for the vet to check for parasites. I got a really nice treat for my careful aim and deposit.

Pup, who is Australian Shepherd and black Labrador, constantly watches Paul as he works except when she plays with me. Paul rescued her from the boring back-yard of a previous owner. Basque shepherds from Spain brought Pup's Shepherd ancestors to the United State more than 200 years ago. Based on an earlier address, they were named Australian by the Americans.

Manners

Once, I swore repeatedly at Tom, our nice UPS man, when he would not let me dance or jump on him. I was banished to my kennel. Fortunately, I can see through the wires all the time. This time, feeling at the end of my tail, I immediately collapsed, with eyes closed. I didn't have a rope.

In the yard, when that fixed, barking German Shepherd jumps up and down behind his chain link fence, I simply keep my mouth shut and ignore him. Even though I am going to be five months old in three days, it seems best to ignore creatures who ask me to bark obscenities. A psychologist said it is best to ignore bad behavior and to praise good behavior. This can drive another dog hoarse and maybe people, too. This gives one an upper paw, since I do not have a hand. After telling my psychologist friend, Arthur Canter, about my lack of manners, here is what he wrote:

May:

Yes, B.F. Skinner was a famous psychologist who did research using pigeons, rats and monkeys in studying the science of behavior. He had a great impact on behavioral science from his wide varieties of research on behavior and animal interrelationships. I am reminded of his basic research on learning when I see pictures of old ladies pulling away at casino slot machine handles to get their rewards of coins. It's just like the pictures of rows of pigeons in their side-by-side stalls pecking madly away to get seeds. In labs the rats press away furiously on the levers that deliver food pellets only once in a while, concluding that "partial reinforcement," even randomly applied, results in very strong habits that are markedly resistant to extinction (unlearning).

So be careful with what you lick that has a satisfying effect, even for a moment or two!

—Arthur Canter, Ph.D.

A Wild Dog

My family began questioning my emotional behavior at 14 weeks. They wonder if I am bi-polar or have a split personality, based on my quickly shifting moods. Dwayne says I am a wild dog when he lets me out of my kennel. I can be very quiet and then playfully bite at my tail. I smile when Dwayne shouts "no biting and no jumping." I would be happy to pose for that mid-century photographer who photographed people jumping, including Salvadore Dali, the artist. It is very hard to remember not to jump on people. Aside from preferring to eat April's dog food, what I like best is to impulsively run. Recently I ran up and down the driveway 15 times before collapsing for seven hours in my kennel.

My mood changes concern my family. Should I be like the rest of America's hyperactive children on drugs, CALMED? Should Joan and Dwayne invest in pharmaceutical stocks to enable all of us to have an economically comfortable old age? There is no Leona Helmsley to leave me many millions when Dwayne and Joan may be put down. They need to think of my future, don't they? Would I still be me if I had to take medicines or does an exhausting run do the same for me? Dwayne believes there may be a problem with depression when I am restrained and whining in my kennel.

A family friend, the late Richard Wiley of Washington, Iowa, a computer expert and farmer, was adopted by a small dog with a Labrador face and a Dachshund body. Now this dog is a subject for psychoanalysis, especially regarding his feelings about his short legs, long body, and soulful face.

Some say anti-depression pills might cause severe memory loss. I'm too young for analysis since my experiences are so limited. I will never have emotional disturbances and questions of whether to fall in love with a French Poodle or a Labrador, and certainly not a Great Dane.

Family friends, noting my soulful eyes and beauty, my energy and exuberance, are asking if I should be considered for adoption and possibly a better home with a younger dog and people under age fifty. A visitor, Arthur Koenig, said, "I had a Labrador and he died. If May needs a home, I will be happy to take her to my place in San Antonio, Texas."

This is one of my favorite hats given to Joan at the time of the Texas copyright lawsuit against Joan and her publishing company.

"Texas? No way," screamed Dwayne and Joan in unison. That is the state where the federal Judge Samuel B. Kent, Galveston, was scheduled to preside over the copyright case against Joan and her company's book, *License to Cook Texas Style,* which allegedly violated the copyrights of another book. The lawyers asked for an estimated $400,000. Copyright, copycat is my attitude even though I have yet to meet a cat. The case got settled at almost the last minute in 2002 thanks to Carol Blakely of Dallas, a recipe expert; Attorney Karen Tripp of Houston; and Attorney Tom Riley of Cedar Rapids, Iowa.

I would prefer to take my chances in Iowa with Dwayne and Joan than move to a state where sometimes dead people get to vote and other strange events happen. Even though Joan said she still loves Texans, I am not to move. Hopefully, Dwayne and Joan will recognize that even though I am a wild dog, I'm just a puppy.

Politics in the Dog Park

Meeting Sophie, a Labradoodle

My social life in winter is isolated from other dogs. Often, I do not even consider myself a dog, but rather as a reincarnation from another life, perhaps as a writer, or maybe even a poet. It is unusual to touch only noses. Usually we sniff the private parts of other dogs. As I gain confidence, I am trying not to go upside down even if the dog is bigger.

As I was trying to kiss two very large white French Poodles (long lost genetic relatives), they barked and viciously chased me.

In desperation, I flattened myself upside down as Dwayne raced to rescue me. When the French Poodles ganged up on me, I reverted to being subservient. That is politics. I do not like the dogfights that break out between the larger dogs. I need to be more like the bossy Pug belonging to the Cileks. Even though she is so tiny, she likes to herd, and does not fight. That is a more graceful route to dominance. (See the photo of Miss Pinky Cilek, page 32.)

Times are changing. It is due to the unrestrained Poodle in me. I am filled with love for all dogs large and small and for all people. I have to stop kissing all the dogs and work for greater integration, tolerance, and understanding, even in the dog park. This is difficult when you think love conquers all, and I prefer black dogs who are mutts like me.

A Lover Propositions

The aristocratic Gus lives with Sue and Paul in Illinois. They are very proud of him. They sent me his photographs. Although he is ten, I hope he is not too experienced. He asked for a two-night stand if we would provide plenty of beer for his drivers. I seriously entertained his offer to visit.

Sending My Photo to Gus

Now that I am over six months old, it seemed like a good idea to let Gus see a current photograph of me with my long tail gaining a beautiful length. While I do not have curls, I do have very attractive waves on my back. Mellow best describes my temperament as I grow more mature. I really love dogs.

Gus Makes a Fatal Mistake

Gus sent me this snapshot of Olive nursing her family of eight puppies sired by Gus.

Standard Poodles are among the most intelligent of dogs. Olive is a black Labrador. Her babies are first generation Labradoodles.

Considered designer dogs, Labradoodles first were created in Australia, mating a French Poodle with a Labrador. They are very popular in America and available in a variety of sizes and colors.

Photos of Gus, Olive and puppies courtesy of Paul Heller and Sue Coles, owners of Gus

The puppies of Gus and Olive are shown on the way to their first visit to the vet. Half of these Labradoodles are black like me. The others are versions of Gus.

Recovery after Surgery

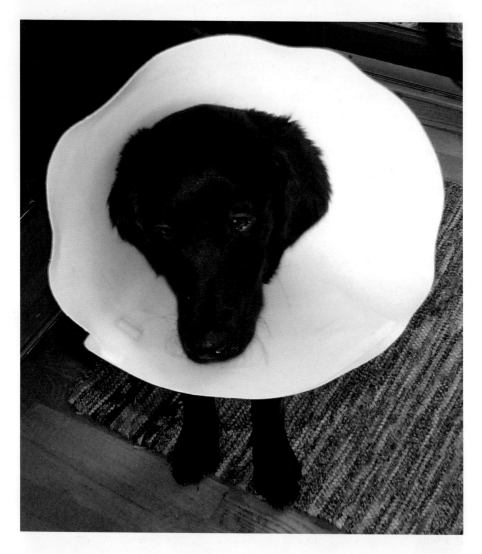

As appealing as Gus might be, I did not want to compete with Olive for his affection, nor do I want such a large family! What about my future? What about my long legs and slim figure? What about my possible career as a New York model? I scheduled a hysterectomy and then, a day later, I had to wear this white halo to avoid scratching you know where! So much for Gus. Thanks, but no thanks!!

A Whisper from April

May, I do not want to talk too loud about this sensitive subject, but before Joan married Dwayne, I got to sleep with her in the bed. Dwayne kicked me out, saying he does not sleep with dogs.

That was in 1996. In the office, I've had to make do ever since: sleeping under an office desk, on a dog bed, or near John Johnson's desk, and even on the cement floor. Just three choices. You might try petitioning Joan and Dwayne to allow you into the bedroom, then to make room for you at the foot of the bed, even though they have to use a flashlight to avoid stepping on you. Eventually you might persuade them to let you become a foot warmer at the end of the bed. Joan has cold feet.

I am enclosing information on research about people who sleep with their dogs. Just surf the Internet. Our mutual friends in McGregor are happy to contribute testimonials about sleeping with their dogs. **Do not tell this to Dwayne. It just gives him ammunition!** Good luck.

—Your sister, April

Bedtime News from the Internet

A major medical clinic is studying patients who sleep with pets. According to a product company's survey, a majority of pet owners sleep with their cats and dogs—and many say their furry companions are better sleep partners than the human variety.

In fact, half of pet owners claim their sleep is disturbed by a human partner, compared to slightly over one-third who claim pooches and pussycats wake them up constantly. Women are more inclined to prefer pets in their bed to men. Over half of the women say men are more of a bed hog than a dog or a cat, and a smaller percentage of men can't decide if a woman or a pet is more inclined to keep them awake at night.

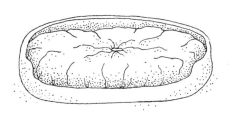

A Letter from Kathy Hall

Here Is The Story of Lou

Shortly after Terry and I moved to our new house in 2002, a friendly black Lab appeared on our doorstep. He was wearing a collar and was named Lou. We called the owner immediately, worried that Lou was lost. Lou's owner Jim, a nice young dentist, showed up quickly and retrieved the dog. As it turns out, Jim lived well over a mile away, but Lou had a direct shot to our house on an old utility trail. We wondered why he chose our house, but figured it was a fluke and didn't expect to see him again.

A few weeks after that, we came home from work to find Lou sunning himself on our deck. This happened with increasing regularity for a few months, and over time we grew very fond of Lou… we didn't hurry quite so much to call Jim, and Jim didn't seem too worried that Lou frequently visited us. My son begged to let Lou in the house, but I refused. We did not need a damn dog in the house, and our three cats would have a fit.

It didn't take long until I caved. It was cold, and Lou was shivering, so I said okay, but he can only come in the garage. Then I let him in the basement, where the old furniture is. He seemed delighted to be indoors, and the cats adored him. Pretty soon he was upstairs and in the living room. Before long he was curled up on the furniture. Eventually he slept in bed with me.

For a few years, we pretty much shared Lou with Jim, and grew to enjoy Jim as well. Our joint custody arrangement was entirely on Lou's terms. When Jim planned his first trip to Europe, he asked if we would mind taking care of Lou while he was gone. We were happy to agree, and made arrangements for Jim to drop him off at our house. Lou showed up alone, three days before expected, and we had a lovely time.

Last winter, we noticed that Lou was visiting much less often. I was at work when Jim called. Lou had cancer, and Jim was on the way to the vet for that last visit. We grieved together and missed the wonderful dog that had become part of all our lives.

Our doorbell rang at Christmastime last year. It was Jim, with a bottle of wine (his traditional gift after one of Lou's extended visits) and a gift bag. He had brought a beautiful framed photo of Lou, and it now sits in a place of honor at my son's apartment.

I guess we can never predict the unexpected pleasures that enter our lives. But one of mine was a wonderful black Lab with wanderlust and an owner who was willing to share him with me.

—Kathy

My Question

About the cats. Did they sleep with you too? You, your husband, the cats and Lou?

Kathy's answer:

"The cats were in bed, too. It was a rotating arrangement, usually with Lou at my feet and assorted cats in between Terry and me. Terry is very patient."

Kathy's photograph of Lou on a porch chair

Pinky Cilek Sends an E-Mail

Hi May,

Thanks for considering my photos. I know I'm irresistible!

My age is no secret. I'm two. I'm extremely proud of my genetics: 75 percent Pug and 25 percent Beagle. It's hard to beat that perfect combination.

I have slept with Shelly, but this is a secret. I'm a little hesitant to admit this but I prefer my cage at night and my blankie. Mums the word on that one.

Love, Pinky

Shelly Cilek photos

The Cost of Raising Me

Dwayne's first cousin sent an e-mail mentioning the cost of having a dog. Here is my response and questions about sleeping habits.

Dear Relative,

My name is May Bourret and I am writing a book, *Finding My Way.* I live with Dwayne and Joan. I am a Labradoodle "reject" without papers. I was very interested in your figures that it will cost more than $16,000 to raise me, and I would like very much to know your source!

Love and licks, May

P.S. Please reply. Dwayne doesn't want you to think I am just wagging with you!

May

Ron's answer:

Dear May:

Welcome to the family. I have no idea where the figures came from; I just pass on what I receive. I've enclosed a picture of Tally and Toby who rule the roost at this Bourret house.

Hope all is well with you. If you ever want to visit Florida, we would love to see you.

Ron Bourret

Dear Cousin,

What kind of dogs are Tally and Toby? I have been collecting testimonials from people who sleep with their dogs and about their experiences. I am petitioning Dwayne and Joan to allow me into their beds, either in McGregor or in Iowa City. Do you and your wife sleep with Tally and Toby?

Love, May

Dear May,

As a follow up: Tally and Toby are Papillons. Yes, they sleep with us as they are inseparable with each other and Jo.

Ron

Ron photographed Tally, left, and Toby Bourret on the Ron and Jo Bourret bed. With a French name meaning butterfly, Papillons came from small Spaniels in Spain and eventually were popular at the court of Louis XIV. The breed has been depicted in frescoes by noted European artists.

My conclusion:

You sure can't trust what people send on the Internet. Although vet services have cost more so far than my folks ever spent in a year for a pediatrician for any of their children, I seriously doubt that it will cost $16,000 for my lifetime. I am picky about the dog food. Nothing imported for me!

My friend Sue Huebsch sent a note that Riley, a Tibetan Terrier, gets to sleep with her the minute her husband Tony leaves the bed. Tony is an early riser.

Note: These dogs guarded their ancestral Lamaist monasteries 2,000 years ago in Tibet. They were never sold, but were given as gifts. A doctor received one in the 1920s and obtained more for breeding. They came to America in 1956, thanks to another doctor and his wife in Montana. Riley may also be related to the Chinese Lhasa Apso.

Mimi Heskje Sleeps Around

May, thanks for wanting photographs of me. I am a Shih Tzu. There are five members in my family. Parents are Eric and Josie Heskje*. Children are Jonah, Lydia, and Levi. I try to sleep where I can find the warmest spot in the house, mainly with Eric on the davenport or with Eric and Josie. When I yawn, the children know it's my time to wander to warmth and love.   *Norwegian name but I am a Mandarin Chinese.

Rejection by Dwayne

When Dwayne examined the black-and-white photographs of people who sleep with their dogs and after reading their stories, he still refuses to let me in the bed with my family. And I'm not allowed in their bedroom. Consequently, I was very depressed.

I do sleep on a little rug by the fireplace in the McGregor home and on a dog bed in the office at the Iowa City home.

I had a dream that maybe if I presented the photographs in color of people who sleep with their dogs, Dwayne would relent! Dogs do see colors, but not as intensely as people see them.

Kim Sends Color Information

October 16, 2008

Dear May,

Our last walk together was fantastic! Autumn colors were peaking and the fresh air and blue sky seemed to help make the world seem right. By the way, you looked especially sleek and shiny romping with your black hair in those yellow leaves. The color contrast was perfect.

Kim Hayes and I share a laugh. She is my therapist and consultant. She understands me. Kim has experience in producing wildlife documentaries in many countries for television and films including IMAX™.

RED stimulates conversation and appetites. It also boosts energy, is warm, alluring, jolly, and tempting. This is why it's used so often in marketing and advertisements to grab people's attention. YELLOW speeds up metabolism, stimulates digestion, and symbolizes spiritual enlightenment and intellect. It's like sunshine. BLUE is calming, peaceful; it's the sky and ocean, expansive and serene. GREEN is the color of nature, and is why we love our walks together; it's the balancing color on the spectrum half way between red and violet. It's equilibrium and relaxation. I know you're chomping at the bone for me to get to BLACK, your favorite color. It represents elegance and sophistication, and can be distinguished or racy. It also represents the color of mourning, which is in keeping with its serious nature.

Doctors, as you've noticed when you went to get your hysterectomy, wear WHITE jackets. While white at first symbolizes cleanliness and purity, it also denotes superiority and can make others feel inadequate or, get this one, ill at ease. Maybe they've been secretly taking advantage of us. Get it, ill at ease and dis-ease, you know, the placebo effect! The next time we walk we can discuss the placebo effect, and you also wanted to talk about some of your past lives. One minute you think I'm nuts talking about color therapy, and the next you have no problem believing in reincarnation and even tell me you remember a few of your past lives.

The Arvidson Family

Dear May,

We have had Ollie for three and one-half years, and Peggy Sue for one and one-half years. Both are Australian Blue Heelers. However, Ollie is a mix of the Blue and Red Heeler coloration. Both dogs are remarkably smart, as is commonly the case with the breed. Ollie knows many tricks, but my wife Patty hasn't had as much time to spend training Peggy. She learns quickly, and is very well behaved.

Ollie, on the other hand, can be a stinker. When we got Ollie, it was understood that she would be an outside dog, would not sleep in the house, and would not receive food scraps from the table. After a few days, perhaps a week, she was sampling our food. When I mentioned that she was getting spoiled, my wife replied, "She is only getting what she deserves."

Being an old softy, I couldn't take issue with this. Soon she was spending nights in the house, but not on the queen-size bed, as I put my foot down on this. For a short while, that is. Once on the bed, she made herself right at home, lying crosswise in the middle. Of course, my wife generally retires before me so she would take her position first, Ollie second, and I got what was left, about two feet on the edge. This became the norm until Peggy Sue arrived. She started out in another room and seemed quite contented, but after a few weeks, she started whimpering at night.

Of course, she needed to sleep on our bed close to her mommy. This created friction between Peggy Sue and Ollie until our new respective positions were established: Patty on one side, Ollie across the foot of the bed, Peggy in the middle and me clinging to the edge. There are times I find no room left for me when I come to bed. I must rearrange the two dogs, which is easier said than done. On the worst nights, I have to contort myself into odd angular positions to fit in, and fight for the covers. We may have to look for a king-size bed pretty soon.

One of our favorite stories is when Ollie was still a pup. She wanted to play ball one night while we were watching television. We told her that we were busy. After a few minutes of being ignored, she walked over to the tube, dropped the ball, pressed the off button with her nose, picked up the ball and looked at us, as if to say "You are going to play with me now,

Jim, Ollie, Peggy Sue and Patty Arvidson

right?" The amazing thing is that we rarely watch television, and very seldom a movie, so how she knew to turn off the set is a complete mystery. But she knew!

It works both ways, however. She used to come to the front door at night barking to come in. When we came to open the door, she would take off running and barking across the lawn. This happened with regularity, so we finally stopped going to the door for her. Then she would come to the window and bark. We would get up and go to the door, and off she would go. So my wife started to get up as usual when she barked at the window, and Patty sat back down when the dog ran to the door. This finally stopped the game. We look forward to many more years of love and fun from both of our dogs. They are our children, "the girls."

—Dr. James Arvidson

A Letter from Belle

Both photographs are by Helen Grunewald

Belle lies on the family bed. Jane is pictured below. They herd sheep for Tom Millward and Helen Grunewald on their Blairstown, Iowa, farm.

Dear May,

I thought I should tell you about the other two dogs that reside in our bedroom. Jane is the first one to have a place on the bed. She spent her first night on the farm crying in the mud room, and she has slept on the bed ever since. Jane is not my sister and has very short hair. When Helen meditates, she lies outside Helen's bathroom. I think Jane was a Buddhist in another lifetime. Tibetans believe that misbehaving nuns and monks are reincarnated as dogs in their next lives.

Jane is working hard for a better rebirth. Jane is a Border Collie like me, but she may have some Blue Heeler. Sean is my brother, a year older, and sleeps at the side of the bed. He is too big and usually too stinky to be on the bed.

Love, Belle

Jane

Sleeping with Our Whippets

By Fred Easker

We've had Whippets for about thirty years. One of the first things one learns about new Whippets is that they have an affinity, no I should say the belief that they are entitled to raised, soft furniture such as beds, sofas and upholstered chairs.

Our first Whippet, Pupper, was six months old when he came to live with us. As soon as his anesthesia wore off (that's another story), he leapt onto our bed. Our second Whippet, Poonie, joined us after a year or so, and since the elder Whippet had no hesitation asserting alpha-male superiority, he kept his place between us. The puppy clung to the tiny space between me and the edge of the bed.

We were much younger then and tolerated being poked by long legs stretching out in the night. For all their visual grace, Whippets aren't so graceful as they slam into one's side at the end of the ritual spiral descent to a snug fetal position.

Years passed and Pupper was no longer with us. He was replaced by Jimi, who was supposed to be our son Jason's dog. Our bed was a little less full with only Poonie. As children head off to college and then on to new jobs, they leave their four-footed friends in the care of those staying behind. We were again back to two dogs.

Jimi learned to crawl under the covers without help. He'd go to the top of the bed, and pushing his nose under the edge of the bedding, he'd snap his head upward, and before the sheets and blankets could settle to the mattress, he'd drop into a curled position and settle snugly into a nap.

Whippets are proportionately long and tall, but not wide. As his nap continued, he'd stretch out on his side, and, at first glance, he became invisible under the covers. Until we got used to it, he often startled us by raising the bedding up when we came into the room. On one occasion a house guest shrieked loudly when she was startled by the moving blankets.

After fifteen years, Poonie passed and we unexpectedly lost Jimi not too long after. A couple of months of Internet searches and phoning brought us eight-week-old Willy. We were adamant that he would not be sleeping on the bed. We brought a small dog crate to the side of the bed, and lined it with soft blankets. On that first night, we carefully placed him inside,

Photograph by Fred Easker

Willy Easker

latched the door and climbed into bed, expecting to recover from the eight hour round trip to get him.

When our son was born, we went through a couple of days of his constant crying until we relaxed, settled into a routine and learned his. But his crying seemed a whisper compared to what came from that dog crate. His was the sound of a baby's cry squeezed through a bagpipe, and it was unrelenting.

I tried talking to Willy. We put on the radio tuned to soft music. We tried the old ticking alarm clock trick my father advocated when we got a Beagle when I was a kid. It didn't work then, and it didn't work in our hour of greatest need. We pushed our heads under the pillows and vowed to outlast the pup. Night one, no sleep, night two, no sleep. By day six, we were exhausted, dragging ourselves to work, irritable with each other and cursing that little dark-eyed devil. I think it was on night seven, I hopped out of bed, fumbled with the latch in the dark, reached in and pulled the pup from the crate. The silence was bliss! Willy and I headed for the daybed in the extra room, which technically wasn't our bed. Needless to say, the pup won!

Willy has not learned to get himself under the covers, but does paw until we hear him. Sometimes in the night he gets hot. We hear him start to pant, lightly at first but slowly building until he bursts out from the foot of the bed, goes to get a drink and then plops on the floor until he gets chilled. Soon he's back on top of the bed, pawing to get in. When we are gone, he paws and nudges the pillows to make a wonderful nest within, reposing in sheer ecstasy in his home.

New News from the Easkers

In May 2008, Willy was put down due to a surprisingly aggressive cancer. His high spirits helped us through some tough times, and we missed his happy greetings, the two-mile daily walks and generally goofy mischief. Velga agreed that we would be getting a pup again sometime, but wanted to wait a while—enjoying not having the responsibility. However, after a month or so, I began to do regular Internet searches. As I saw the many possibilities in Whippet coloration, I decided that I wanted one that was marked different from our previous Whips and finally decided that black would be the predominate color. Black Whippets are not so plentiful, apparently, because they don't show so well. Then one day a guy called Devo showed up on a Website. I was in Lansing and forwarded the picture to Velga with the note that this was the one. A few days later, after we discussed temperament with the breeder on the phone, we decided to go get him.

The Friday after Thanksgiving we headed to the Pittsburgh area, spent Saturday visiting the Carnegie Museum and the Andy Warhol Museum and had a great day with clear skies and warm temperatures, all the while keeping our eye on the promised bad weather. Sunday morning we drove in the rain to rural New Brighton, picked up Devo and headed home. All day we drove through lots of rain and the kind of snow that sticks to the grass but not the road. When we got past Chicago, we had some nasty weather and very slow driving, but got home okay.

Newly named Jackson, this action Whippet has settled in nicely—potty

Fred and Velga Easker pictured above at their Lansing studio are noted artists. Fred paints landscapes of the river and lands in Eastern Iowa. Velga creates quilt patterns out of found objects such as the cancelled stamp featuring a detail from the painting Young Corn *by Grant Wood.*

Velga Easker photograph

Fred holds Jackson. He is the namesake of famous artist Jackson Pollock. Whippets and Greyhounds are related.

training is going well, and he's already learned a couple of simple tricks.

When he is not ripping up newspapers and playing with his tug toys or doing "zoomies" back and forth in our upstairs hall, he prefers to be in a lap, where he is as I write. We're not getting much work done. So far he has not asked to sleep with us.

Rogeta Halvorson rescued Joe Joey Cocker at a shelter in Dallas. They now live and sleep together in McGregor, Iowa. The Cocker Spaniel breed was developed in Great Britain.

A Sleepover at Dianne and Carl's Home
Knoxville, Tennessee

Dear May,

The arm in the photo is mine. The large black-and-white dog is Mac, a rescue from South Carolina. At 13, Mac is a prefect pal.

The little tan-and-white is Monty, my sweet baby. We found this Jack Russell three years ago while on a horseback ride near Union County, Tennessee. This little guy played us from the moment he saw us. He was sweet and gentle, and after riding with us for over an hour, allowed me to leash him and place him in our truck, where he slept for the long ride home. He was perfect for a few days, then we had to leave for a ten-day trip.

We came back to a reign of terror! I began to refer to him as the Son-of-Satan, and understood why his previous owner didn't search for him. I seriously offered people large amounts of money to please take him. They snickered. Now, after obedience and agility classes, vigorous exercise, much socialization, and an endless sense of humor, we adore the little trickster.

John, our latest red-neck, hillbilly, coon-mutt puppy rescue, is not yet in our bed, but he is making Monty's first year seem like a cakewalk! What in the—multiple four-letter words plus a few colorful Spanish ones—was I thinking? Some of us never learn! The gray fur ball is Lucy, our queen cat rescue.

—Dianne Inchausegui Thompson

Photograph by Dr. Carl Thompson

Sleeping with Wirehaired Fox Terriers Skipper and Willow

Skipper, Anne Loomis, Chuck Boeder, and Willow
These dogs have English heritage.

A Message to May

By Anne Loomis

I tell you, I HAVE slept with some dogs in my life, but I'm guessing you're talking about the canines and not the human dogs...

I sleep with two badly behaved Terriers; the male is Skipper and the female is Willow. Willow and Skipper, just like other beings who reside together, have a complex relationship.

They are frequently trying to decide "who made you the boss of me?" (Which in law school was called Civil Procedure.) Willow deeply believes that the bed, and everything else in the house, for that matter, is hers.

Skipper is not on board with that theory and disregards Willow's position. He isn't into controlling Willow, and resists the notion that she can control him.

Therefore, going to bed is sometimes a complex issue. If Willow gets to bed first, she crouches at the edge and prepares to defend with growling and a show of teeth (I'm sure you are well acquainted with "display"). If I'm not in bed to lend aid, Skipper may just wait until I get there. If I'm there, he will board the bed just behind me for protection from She Who Must Be Obeyed.

Arranging ourselves is another negotiation. Generally, Skipper gets to sleep next to me, or when Chuck is home, between us. The warmer he is, the happier, and between the two humans is the absolute best for warmth.

Willow prefers to be on lookout at the foot of the bed. I'm not sure what Willow is defending us from—have the Chi Coms threatened our borders? Undocumented workers? Whatever the noise, you can be sure it will immediately put Willow on her feet defending with ear-piercing barks. I told Chuck the other day when Willow paces around the house in a paranoid manner looking for the various threats she knows are lurking, she looks a bit like Richard Nixon. Possibly she has already planted the bugs to gather surveillance. Well, there you go. For people who don't sleep with dogs, they no doubt cannot comprehend why I go to such trouble. It's more than just the warmth of a warm puppy by your side; it's feeling like being a member of the pack. I only wish they'd let me be the boss, but I'm working on that.

A Friend Sends An E-Mail

May, how wonderful to see your family on Wednesday night at the Kirkwood dinner! I told everyone at our table about your upcoming book—we're all dog sleepers—we had Chihuahuas, Border Collies, Jack Russell Terriers, and a Labrador. I come from a whole family of dog sleepers—my sister Anne has Border Collies, Nikki has two Jack Russells, and I've got dear Bob the Chihuahua and Casper who is a mutt.

—Kayt Conrad

Lucy, a Golden Retriever, sleeps with Jeff and Jeni White. Lucy loves head gear. Here she is in a Harley-Davidson cap. Lucy claims British ancestry, with relatives in Canada, Australia, and most of Europe.

Lucy sends holiday greetings to her many friends.

My Life, Dakota and Lady

Randy Sandersfeld with Siberian Huskies Dakota and Lady

Hi May,

When I spent time in Hollywood, I worked in an office with Demi Moore. The place was called "Hollywood Video." She sat behind a desk eating sunflower seeds all day, and occasionally answering the phone. I worked the night shift in the back room, making tapes of old movies like

"Citizen Kane." I ran into Demi a couple of years later on the set of General Hospital, and we chatted for a while. That show was her first big break. It was my first teeny break, and as big as it would get.

I was a hack driver in New York City (horse and carriage), giving people rides through Central Park until the wee hours of the morning. I spent four-plus years as a flight attendant.

Finally I moved back to my hometown of Amana, Iowa. I have a small tree business, "Out on a Limb." I am the owner and the only employee. (I'm not too hard on myself.)

I met Lady in Austin, Texas. An ex-convict, who was living out of his pickup, had her tied to his front bumper (only when it was parked). He would travel around from festival to festival, with six Shetland ponies he made into a merry-go-round on which he would give little kids rides, and then charge them extra to take their pictures. I waved some money in his face, and Lady was mine. (Lady was the name he had given her, and that's the only reason I kept it.)

Dakota (blue eyes) is Lady's pup. Dakota had a brother, Rocky, that was shot and killed by a neighboring farmer for no reason at all. That was the worst day of my life. In Cedar Rapids, Channel 9 News did the story. Since then I've just heaped more love onto Lady and Dakota; what else can you do? I did start a blog-site (http://farewelltorocky.blogspot.com) which has the news story, the editorial I wrote and the song I wrote for Rocky. People can also leave a comment.

The other day we went to the dog park in Iowa City. There were a few inches of snow on the ground. Dakota acted like a sinner that got to spend the next half-hour in heaven. Her feet barely touched the ground. I think I had as much fun as she did. Well, that's just another of the wonders and joys only a dog lover knows.

It's just us now; we're one happy little family keeping each other cozy on a queen-size futon.   —Randy Sandersfeld

Editor's note: Randy is active in Amana's Iowa Theatre Artists Company.

The Siberian Husky was developed as a sled dog by nomadic people of Northeast Asia. These dogs became famous for racing across Alaska to deliver Nome residents serum for diptheria in 1925. They served in World War II in the U.S. Army search-and-rescue teams.

Chase Barnett, age twelve, of Houston, sent his photograph and a note that says he begins every night sleeping with Star, an eight-year-old Cavalier King Charles Spaniel, his very own dog. Here Star kisses Chase. This breed is named for Charles II of England, Scotland, and Ireland (1630-1685). They are related to Pugs. The family, also, has Sandy Pumroy, a fourteen-year-old Golden Retriever, who sleeps alone.

Karen Tripp photograph

Cocoa, a Coonhound-Collie mix, sleeps with her owner, Gary Dahnke of Coralville, Iowa. When he went to the farm to interview a litter of pups a few months old, twenty pound Cocoa selected Gary by following him around. Now 55-pounds, she takes most of the bed and leaves a small area on the edge for Gary. Her life is that of a pet, not a hunter. Collies are British. Coonhounds were bred in Appalachia and the Ozarks as hunters.

Milo, a sixty-pound Vizsla, recommends the good life in California.

Dear Milo,

Thanks for your photograph and e-mail inviting me to the West Coast. It is great you get to sleep in bed with your owners, Larry Canter and Patty Dunlap, at your home in Healdsburg! How wonderful that Larry takes you for a good run at Sea Ranch. Larry and Patty are my kind of people!!!

Love and licks, May

Learn about Milo's ancestry and favorite treat on page 110.

A Friend for Naps

Ruth Heffner and Daphne, a standard French Poodle, nap together and often share a bed. Ruth and her husband, Ray, rescued Daphne, age nine, from an animal shelter three years ago. They actually have two dogs. Their aging Golden Retriever, Luke, cannot get on the bed due to arthritis. Ruth has a friend who sleeps with five rescued dogs. Every time they lose a dog due to old age, they find another one in need at a shelter the very next day. "It is the only way we can survive the loss," Ruth said.

Lynette Etzel and Sophie

Lynette Etzel photo

*Allie and
Sophie*

Our Shi-Poo, Sophie, a mixture of Shih Tzu and a Poodle, was born on December 15, 2006. We bought her at a pet store. They had lots of puppies, but she caught my eye and heart. It was love at first sight. My husband, Steve, wasn't excited about having two dogs but went along with it. I really wanted a dog to cuddle with, and I got my wish. She's been a good addition to our family. Allie, our Siberian Husky, who has one brown eye and one blue eye, and Sophie love to wrestle. They get along great. Sophie is 12 pounds and Allie is 90 pounds. We thought Allie would be under 50 pounds. She would sleep with us if we allowed it. Two dogs crowd the bed. Sophie's origins are Tibetan and French.　　　　　—Lynette Etzel

Bob, Susie, and Candi Moran on their houseboat deck on the Mississippi River. As a miniature Poodle and Bichon, Candi's origins are French and Mediterranean, going back thousands of years.

Bob sent this letter about life with Candi.

Candi came to us at about one year of age from a rescue pound in Fertile, Iowa. Susie responded to an advertisement seen on the Internet by a friend of hers. Candi is half miniature Poodle and the other half may be Bichon. She is nine years old and 18 pounds. We had been without canine companionship for about 1-1/2 years prior to her arrival.

She loves us so much that she allows us sole use of "her" bed after the light goes out at about 11:30. She remains out of the communal quarters until after 5:00 A.M., when she wakes up Bob to receive her morning head petting and full back stroking. Candi then hops up to the foot of the bed and makes her way to Bob's pillow to snuggle down between us—many times lying so as to give nice pressure between Bob's shoulder blades, which really feels great. When Susie wakes up and takes the middle spot, Candi has to move to the other side. That should be a good location (but not preferred) as Candi will now have half the bed. Bob never gets more than one-fourth to one-third of the bed.

Candi loves to travel and does anything just to be with us. She only fears a fly swatter. She must have been swatted as a pup; she has the memory of an elephant. When in Cedar Rapids, Candi frequently spends time with her best friend, Molly, Susie's mom's Shih Tzu. On summer weekends she enjoys her third family on the Mississippi by going over to the boat next door and sitting quietly by the door until they open it for her to come in. Treats are frequently involved. She minds well if it is in her best interest. Best dog we ever had.

My neighbors the Bickels, John (Corky) and Mary Ellen (Med), found that a queen-size bed was not large enough to accommodate two full grown Portuguese Water Dogs (PWD) plus themselves. Rather than Corky and Med sleeping on the floor, they bought a king-size bed. They have had a number of sets of PWDs, forerunner to the Poodle and Irish Water Spaniel, and no doubt distant relatives of mine.

The PWDs in this photograph are Whipsie Mae, left, and Rio with the white paw.

Editor's Note: Whipsie Mae and Rio's ancestors may have come to Portugal with the fifth century Visigoths or later with the Moors. After a stay in England, they came to the United States in the 1950s.

Monty Crum, a Cairn Terrier, wrote suggesting an appealing alternative to my request to sleep in the bed with Joan and Dwayne. One of Monty's relatives was the featured dog in The Wizard of Oz.

Dear May,

I am very careful on the leather furniture of my owners, Don and Dorothy Crum. I know you want to sleep in the same bed with Dwayne and Joan, but have you thought of asking them if you can sit on furniture and sleep there, too? Maybe they would rather have you on furniture than in the bed?

My niece, Hanna, named me Monty because all her dogs have names beginning with M. She has two Collies, Madeleine and Max, and a Bichon named Molly. At least they have each other. Since I have no play-mates at home, Don takes me two mornings a week to a dog play place. We have many parties and some of the dogs wear costumes for Halloween and on Valentine's Day. I wish you could go with me.

Love, Monty

Pam White sleeps with Hansel, foreground, and Gretel, 190 pounds of Weimaraners. Pam confided to me that "my sleeping with both dogs for seven years was a factor in my most recent divorce. The dogs and I are very happy now."

Note: These dogs trace ancestry to the court of Grand Duke Karl August of Weimar in Germany and were developed as gun dogs to hunt large game.

Pastor Bill Eckhardt, holding Shinko, a Maltese whose full name is Prushinko, wears the 1882 attire worn by professional men of the era. Shinko's ancestry comes from the Island of Malta.

Pastor Bill says, "I refuse to own up to sleeping with Shinko, but it is difficult for me to deny it has happened...especially when you find a small warm spot in the bed." He asks, "Who is in control? Humans or the dogs?" Pastor Bill has been summoned by people calling about a death in the family. Upon arriving, Pastor Bill found the death was that of the family dog. His answer: "Some say no, but heaven is a wonderful place, and dogs make a lot of places wonderful. I can't imagine heaven without puppy dogs with Christian charity and forgiveness. We owe them so much. I thank God on a regular basis for two most practical gifts: dogs and naps."

When my sister April died, I called Pastor Bill to come.

In Remembrance of April
1995 – 2008

Obituary

April Liffring-Zug Bourret, age 13, died gracefully June 6, at 10 a.m. at the All Pets Vet Clinic in Iowa City. She could no longer walk without falling.

A Tribute to April

April gradually adjusted to my living with her, mainly because Dwayne and Joan always fed her first in her own bowl. From ages twelve to thirteen (ninety-one plus in dog years), it is a bit difficult enduring a puppy trying to play. April barked to scold me. In her last few months, she had great difficulty standing and walking, and she had cataracts. The next to last night of her life, she let me sleep right beside her, and I kept licking her face, giving all the Poodle love I had to give and more.

Her final morning she could not stand without falling. John Johnson and Dwayne carried her to the van, and Dwayne drove her to the vet. There in a private room, Dwayne patted goodbye and then April scooted with help to Joan who had raised her from puppyhood in the fifteen months before Dwayne came into their lives. Dwayne left the room and Joan and April had a private ten minute goodbye with pats and memories. Soon April was at peace. She had always been stoic about shots, and I follow her example to quietly accept whatever a vet offers me.

We have her ashes to sprinkle in the wildflower garden by our family and friends memorial bench next to the Mississippi River. April's name will be engraved on a stone from northern Minnesota. This kind of rock is one of the oldest in the world, dating from when millions of years ago, the earth was forming. April's rock will be placed next to the memorial bench in McGregor. Out of respect for April, I have not eaten out of her special bowl for two months.

When the ashes of family friend Ruth Nash were sprinkled near the memorial bench, Dwayne read a poem by Ruth. Then, Dwayne and Joan and two people from the Mississippi River Museum in Dubuque, who had known Ruth, walked back to our house. April, however, wanted to check out the ashes and soon emerged from dead flowers and shrubs covered with Ruth Nash's white ashes. Ruth had been a friend of April.

Condolences came by e-mail after Joan sent out this notice to friends of April, an obedient and beautiful dog. We gave her Christmas stockings to a little girl named April.

From cousin Dr. Peter Lucke, Alliance, Ohio:

Here are some photographs I took one afternoon in 2006. April and I walked down to the river and back. While April and I were resting I discovered a beautiful lily nearby. (The lily is in color on page 65.)

April took one of her final swims in the Mississippi River, emerging with sand mixed in her black coat.

From April's Baby Book

Six-week-old April, a Border Collie-Labrador mix, is held by Jordan, age ten, son of Aunt Carol and Uncle David of Amana who now own Rebel. Dog in the foreground is the late Hershey, their family dog who was put down at age thirteen. She is a mix of German Shepherd and Beagle. Before I was born, Jordan was killed at age nineteen by a reckless driver, and Uncle David was injured severely in the crash. Jordan loved dogs. I grieve with all his family over losing him five years ago. Grief and the memories of Jordan and his kindness to all remain forever in our family.

Posing for My Modeling Career

I will rise above Dwayne's rejection of having me in his bed, but one result of my showing him the photographs in color of dogs who sleep with owners is that I can sleep in their bedroom on a dog bed. When I want to get him up, I gently kiss his face and lay my head on his arm. I now need a portfolio of my very best poses for a New York modeling career. Here I am sitting on Dwayne's Norwegian *kubbestol* carved by Phillip Odden of Barronett, Wisconsin. Please, note my long graceful legs.

I was very attracted to Mary Jane Ferguson at the 2008 McGregor Labor Day parade and asked her if she could come for coffee at our home and pose with her awesome hat. She goes to Red Hat Society® meetings.

I would enjoy attending Red Hat Society® luncheons.

There are many choices of products for members of the Red Hat Society®
for women over fifty. I will not qualify for membership for several years,
since I am under two in dog years, about ten in human years.

I like this turban style.

I would rather model sumac than fig leaves anytime.

This hat reminds me of how very patriotic I feel. I do not run with terror-
ist dogs. In fact, I do not know any. I may have been a pacifist in an earlier life.

I would rather model hats than bikinis!

A friend sent me this foxy hat from Canada in hopes that my modeling career can be international. I don't know if the animal rights activists should see this photograph. Save the wolf groups might want the foxes preserved for the wolves.

My friend, Donna Staples, a beautician at Country Clippers in McGregor, supplied the colorful imported scarf from Korea shown on the page at right. I would like to chew it. Although an import, frankly, I prefer everything made in America!

Everyone in my family loves flowers. Membership in the Sierra Club is important to all of us.

Rhinestones from my Aunt Dede make her a best friend.

Pearls on black are always fashionable. Here, I've added old collectible costume jewelry.

Ready for graduation! But graduation from where? My friend, editor Deb Schense, found this dress for her dog Molly Sue at a secondhand store. Deb, who is in her early forties, explains, "For four bucks, I thought I would dress her up. My other dog, Buster, wore a fine chiffon blue. I was inspired by the TV show *Desperate Housewives* and dressed up Molly Sue to mow the backyard." Who has more fun than Iowans? Without mountains and oceans, the people I know have to create their own entertainment. To see Molly Sue mowing, along with her dog treat recipe, go to page 109.

I don't really feel comfortable having a lot of skin showing, but just in case the only opportunity for me is to model in skin flicks or revealing magazines such as *Playboy*, this shows a great deal of me. I am proud of my impressive legs. Forget the two rows of nipples.

I am not so sure blondes have more fun.

I would like to model for Harley-Davidson ads and to ride a Harley all over the world to visit the countries where the different breeds of dogs shown in my book originated. Historians say we are descendants of wolves. There are illustrations of dogs in cave paintings, in Egyptian art and in Mayan art. Whatever the genetic source of our beginnings, we now love human beings and want to help them in every way possible. My friend Lucy lent me her hat. Her owners ride a Harley.

My photographic modeling portfolio is now ready for submission to New York City agencies. I am eager to chase big apples.

Rejection and Depression

I sent many copies of my portfolio to New York modeling agencies. All rejected me as "Corn Tassel." That is what the girls called Joan's aunt, a pianist from Iowa when she attended The Juilliard School in New York City in the 1920s. I understand her feelings. The hurt Aunt Madeleine suffered echoes to me ninety years later. Of course, I am from west of the Hudson River, but doesn't the Father of Waters, the Mississippi River, count for something? I'm extremely depressed and have spent useless days.

There was the rejection from the East Coast Weimaraners' Syndicate! Those dogs have the market blitzed in calendars, exhibitions, books and more! They must eat steak daily. I lost my chance to be a mother with Gus, rejection from Dwayne to keep me out of "their" bed, although I am now allowed to sleep at the foot of their bed, thanks to the color photos.

I pout and choose to sleep away from Joan and Dwayne by guarding the office or front door. Now that my career as a model in the fashion industry is blocked, what can I do to be of service to others? I was pondering the boredom of my fate, when I met a most unusual visitor who lives a few blocks from our Mississippi River home.

Laughter Yoga for Dogs

The Rev. Laura Gentry, a Lutheran minister who lives in McGregor, came with the suggestion that I offer laughter yoga to dogs through my book and www.penfieldbooks.com. She would guide me. Rev. Laura is a certified laughter yoga teacher. I was so excited and thrilled I could not resist jumping up on her in spite of my training. She didn't seem to mind. We danced, laughed, and frolicked together on the lawn. I knew then and there that I liked laughter yoga.

Laughing Laura's Qualifications

Laura Gentry, or "Laughing Laura," has been a laughter yoga professional since 2006. She founded the Iowa School of Laughter Yoga and has trained people from around the country in the method of laughter yoga. Laughing Laura gives motivational talks, even health care conferences at the Mayo Clinic.

Laughing Laura was invited to participate in a laughter yoga session with Oprah's Emmy Award winning make-up artist, Reggie Wells. The piece aired live on *The Oprah Show* in April 2007.

As a producer, Laura created a laughter yoga film for children called *"Laughter Friends,"* recommended by the American Library Association. She also produced a spoken word CD called *Laugh Your Way There: a Laughter Yoga Workout for Commuters,* and *Today Is a Laughing Day,* an album of laughter songs for kids and kids at heart. The founder of laughter yoga, Dr. Madan Kataria, awarded her for the creative contributions she is making to world laughter by selecting her to be the recipient of the prestigious title of "Laughter Ambassador."

Photography by the Rev. William Gentry

Laughing Laura brought Dr. Ha the gelotologist to meet me.

The study of laughter is called gelotology, which comes from the Greek word "gelos," meaning laughter. Laura tells me she has become healthier due to more laughter in her life. Those who study laughter are gelotologists.

More About Laughter Yoga, Including Laughter Yoga for Dogs

By Laughing Laura

Laughter yoga is a unique phenomenon, which is blazing a happy trail across the globe. This method of merriment was developed by a medical doctor from India in 1995 for the purpose of boosting physical and emotional health through laughter. This movement has gained formidable force and now boasts well over 6,000 clubs in over 60 countries worldwide.

The basic concept of laughter yoga is that anyone can laugh. You don't need jokes, comedy or even a sense of humor. People find this notion a bit difficult to grasp, as they are accustomed to laughter springing from a comic source. Dogs, on the other hand, are naturally experts at this and have never needed jokes to become elated. They simply live in the moment and experience joy throughout their whole bodies as evidenced by their happy faces and wagging tails.

In a laughter yoga session, we initiate laughter as an exercise, and it becomes real and contagious because we make eye contact with one another and cultivate a childlike playfulness. Again, this is an easy task for a dog who always connects with playfulness, especially in puppyhood.

The doctor who developed it, Madan Kataria, called it laughter yoga because the laughter exercises are enhanced by deep yoga breathing. This breath work increases the net oxygen to the body and brain. Dogs, as we know by their panting, are fabulous breathers—true yogis at heart.

Laughter yoga is based on the fascinating scientific fact that the body can't tell the difference between real and fake laughter. Either way, you will get the same physiological and biochemical changes and the same health benefits including a reduction in stress, a boosted immune system, stronger heart health, natural pain relief, and an elevated mood. Gelotologists have conducted studies on humans verifying this claim.

What has not been done by these gelotologists, however, is to study the effects of laughter on dogs. It seems a moot point because dogs never fake their laughter, choosing instead to live more genuinely, authentically. Thus, we can assume that dogs also gain the same set of health benefits as human beings do from laughing. It is for these reasons that I offer to become your laughter coach.

As a puppy, you were in excellent health and spirits. Your exuberance is breathtaking still, and so I found you to be the perfect laughter student. Engaging in any laughter exercise will incite you to great climaxes of joy. May, you are well trained and will not attack your fellow laughers as a less polite dog might. The more laughers, the better for you.

Another component of the laughter yoga method is to speak in gibberish. This allows us to make up our own words to express ourselves. Gibberish, you see, is our native language. Sometimes, adults lose touch with the ability to express their emotions in this uncontrolled way. Speaking in gibberish in a group can help loosen them up so they can truly free their minds and help them to emote and then to laugh more wholeheartedly.

Not all dogs speak gibberish. Some older dogs have lost their interest in such childish games and will simply walk away when offered a gibberish conversation. May, you on the other hand, can become an expert gibberish speaker. When I first spoke to you in gibberish in your puppyhood, you were so elated that you threw yourself onto my lap and started kissing me. I can tell an excited potential student when I see one.

It is my hope that you and your family will practice laughter yoga and gibberish. You will continue to be a happy and healthy dog if you engage in laughter exercises and deep breathing regularly. Furthermore, it will help you to spread joy with even greater skill and commitment to the other dogs you know.

Editor's note: Recent researchers studying the therapeutic benefits of laughter included two doctors at Loma Linda University in California: Dr. Lee Berk and Dr. Stanley Tan.

The Rev. Laura kindly offered to let me try on some of her props used in her laughter lectures and to lend me other items from her extensive wardrobe.

Laura majored in music and drama in college. I need more experience.

Why laugh? Because laughter is good medicine.
Studies say that laughter has the following benefits:
• Reduces stress
• Strengthens and balances the immune system
• Releases endorphins to naturally relieve pain
• Burns calories
• Lowers blood pressure
• Nurtures creativity
• Improves brain function

- Fosters relaxation and better sleep
- Reduces risk of heart disease
- Connects people
- Boosts happiness

Amazingly, laughter can do all that! A gelotologist says that if you bottled all the healthy effects of laughter into a pill, you'd need FDA approval. It is that powerful; it is free and has no side effects.

Laughing Laura is committed to increasing world happiness one laugh at a time.

I would rather have antlers than a chicken on top of my head.

Laughter Exercises for Dogs

For all dog owners, I want to share some laughter exercises I learned from my laughter coach, Laura. When our human companions engage in these activities, their dog friends will follow and both will get an excellent workout for mind, body, and spirit.

Ants in your Pants Laughter - Pretend that ants have invaded your pants. Wiggle and run around grabbing your bottom and laughing hysterically.

Bouncing Laughter - Bounce around on one foot laughing.

Chicken Laughter - Impersonate a wacky chicken until it cracks you and your dog up.

Conga Line Laughter - Make a conga line with your dog. Dance around with the conga tune, singing with a "ha" sound. Be sure to kick your legs out at the end of each measure.

Handshake Laughter - Shake your dog's hand and laugh. Try shaking both hands at once while laughing.

Drop Dead Laughing - Laugh so hard you fall down on the ground and roll around laughing. Be sure your dog rolls around with you.

Full Moon Laughter - Howl at the moon together until it cracks you up. This works best on a full moon night.

Head Patting Laughter - Pat your dog's head, giving it a gentle fluff while laughing.

Hearty Laughter - Raise both arms to the sky. Tilt your head back a bit and laugh as if it were coming up from your toes.

Jell-O® Laughter - Wiggle and giggle like you are Jell-O®.

Laughter Cream - Rub imaginary laughter cream all over yourself and your dog and laugh.

Laughter Leaps - Run forward while making an "oooh" sound and then leap with a big laugh.

Library Laughter - Sit down with your dog and be quiet for a moment. Then pretend you have a case of the giggles, but you are in the library so try to keep it down. Laugh quietly and say "shhh!" like you are trying to be quiet.

Peanut Butter Laughter - Pretend your tongue is stuck to the roof of your mouth because of peanut butter. Laugh about it!

Static Electric Laughter - Pretend that everything you touch gives you a tiny shock of static electricity and makes you laugh. Run around playfully shocking your dog and laughing.

Wide Mouth Laugh - Open your mouth as wide as you possibly can, then walk around laughing that way.

My Favorite Recipes: Homemade Treats

Laura emphasized to me that laughter is easily shared and it is free. She said this is a good career move for me since I am naturally very upbeat. She also told me that having a dog helps people live happier, longer lives. This is very encouraging.

My friends, Kim Hayes and Deb Schense, and their dogs Buster and Molly Sue offered to share some of their favorite treat recipes with me. All are kitchen and dog tested.

My Favorite: Kim's Dog Biscuits

3-1/2 cups unbleached all-purpose
  flour
2 cups whole-wheat flour
1 cup rye flour
2 cups bulgur
1 cup cornmeal
1/2 cup instant non-fat dry milk
  powder

4 teaspoons salt
1 envelope active dry yeast
1/4 cup warm water
3 cups chicken broth
1 egg, slightly beaten
  with 1 teapoon milk

Preheat oven to 300 degrees F. Mix first seven ingredients in a large bowl. Dissolve yeast in warm water (110–115 degrees) in separate bowl. Add to dry ingredients. Add broth, stir till dough forms. Roll out dough to 1/4 inch thickness. Cut out bone or people shapes. Place on greased cookie sheet. Brush with egg/milk glaze. Bake 45 minutes. Turn oven off. Biscuits should remain in oven overnight to harden.

Makes 30 large bones or 60 to 90 smaller biscuits.

Photograph by Deb Schense

Molly Sue, part Britney Spaniel, left, and Buster, a Border Collie-Beagle, highly recommend these recipes created by their owner, Deb Schense.

Buster's Favorite Biscuits

1-1/2 cups flour
3/4 cup oatmeal
1/4 cup cornmeal
1/4 cup peanut butter

1/4 cup vegetable oil
1/4 cup honey
1 teaspoon baking powder
1/2 cup water

Preheat oven to 325 degrees F. Combine all ingredients together slowly. Mix well on low. Place one large spoonful at a time onto ungreased cookie sheet. Flatten to 1/4 inch with the tines of a fork. You can bake larger cookies and later cut them into smaller pieces after cooling. Bake at 325 degrees for 15–20 minutes, or until golden brown. Makes 20 big biscuits.

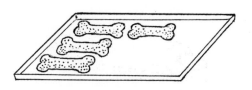

Desperate Dog Lives photography by Deb Schense

Some dogs chase cars. Molly Sue goes all out to mow the lawn in her spare time. No animals were harmed in the making of this photo.

Molly Sue's Desperate Dog Delights

2 cups unsifted flour
1-1/4 cups shredded Cheddar
2 cloves garlic, minced

1/2 cup salad oil
4 to 5 tablespoons water

Mix first four ingredients in a food processor until coarsely chopped. Add just enough water until mixture will form into a ball. Roll dough to a 1/2 inch thickness and cut into small treat-sized squares. Bake at 400 degrees F for 10–15 minutes. Cool on racks. Store in sealed bags in the refrigerator.

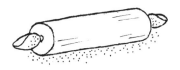

Rebel's Biscuit Recipe

2 cups whole-wheat flour
2 cups all-purpose flour
3/4 cup cornmeal
4 tablespoons vegetable oil
4 bouillon cubes

2 tablespoons bacon drippings
2 cups boiling water

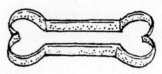

Preheat oven to 300 degrees F. Blend first four ingredients in a large bowl. Mix well. Dissolve bouillon cubes and bacon drippings in boiling water. Stir until dissolved. Add liquid to flour mixture. Mix until it forms a stiff dough. Flatten the dough out on a floured surface. Cut out shapes with a cookie cutter or a drinking glass. Bake at 300 degrees for 30 minutes. Cool on wire racks. Leave overnight to dry, preferably out of Fido's reach.

May's Dog Treat Recipe

3 cups whole-wheat flour
1-1/2 cups bran flakes
1/2 cup instant cooking oatmeal
1 teaspoon salt
1/2 cup bacon drippings

2 eggs, beaten
1 cup milk
1/2 cup peanut butter
1/4 cup honey

Mix first four dry ingredients. Add remaining ingredients. Roll dough to a 1/2 inch thickness on a lightly floured board. Cut into small 1 to 2 inch squares. Place squares on cookie sheet. Bake at 350 degrees F for 20 minutes.

A Special Chicken Treat

Larry Canter prepares chicken thighs for Milo, a Vizsla, by coating them heavily with dry Italian seasoning and roasting them for about an hour at 400 degrees, until they are done and the skin is crispy. He cuts them off the bone (leaving skin on) and then cuts them into small pieces and mixes with regular dog food. Milo has two chicken thighs daily. Because of all the exercise Milo gets, he is very lean and at 5 years old is still on puppy food, which is higher in calories than the adult variety.

Milo's Vizsla ancestors were Hungarian hunting dogs who came with their owners to America and other countries after World War II.

Epilogue

In *Finding My Way*, I have learned the importance of being of service to others. In addition to providing laughter yoga lessons for dogs and recipes for treats, it is my hope that this book will be used as a fund-raiser for animal shelters. Many of the dogs shown here were rescued by shelters. While I am not intimately associated with cats, I do know that shelters provide a great service to them, too. For this reason, I call your attention to the late Vivian Buchan's book listed below, also released by my publisher. My best wags and love to all of you.   —May

Books and Laughter Resources by Mail

$14.95 *Finding My Way* (this book)

$12.95 *Cat Astrology* by Vivian Buchan
This volume shows cat lovers how astrological signs affect their pets. Delightful book. Size 6x9″, 128 pages

Laughter CDs and DVD by Laura Gentry

$14.95 *Laugh Your Way There*
A Laughter Yoga Workout for Commuters CD with laughter exercises for people on the go.

$14.95 *Today is a Laughing Day*
CD of original, jazzy laughter songs for kids and kids at heart

$14.95 *Laughter Friends*
A Laughter Yoga Workout for Commuters DVD High-impact aerobic laughter workout for kids ages 4 to 11. Recommended by the American Library Association.

Shipping and handling $6.95 Iowa residents add 7% Sales Tax
Penfield Books   215 Brown Street, Iowa City, Iowa 52245
1-800-728-9998   www.penfieldbooks.com   Prices subject to change.

Hard is the heart that loveth not in May.

—Chaucer

Hard is the heart that loveth not May.

—Julie Jensen McDonald

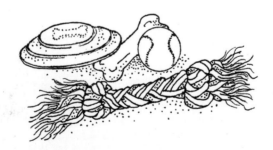